D0606143

'Twas the Night Before ROUND-UP

Written by
Nancy Garhan Attebury

Illustrated by
Joan Gilbert Madsen

Mt. Emily Press

'Twas the Night Before Round-Up
Text copyright ©2009 by Nancy Garhan Attebury
Illustration copyright ©2009 by Joan Gilbert Madsen
First edition 2009

Summary: Four young cowkids wait for the legend of pre Round-Up night to begin. When it does, they end up participating in several rollicking rodeo events while a cheering crowd bolsters their enthusiasm!

ISBN: 978-0-9819940-0-0 (hardcover)
Subjects: Pendleton Round-Up. Rodeo.
Western celebration. Sporting contest.

Library of Congress Control Number: 2009905297
Printed in the United States

Cover and book design by Joan Gilbert Madsen,
j.creative, Enterprise, Oregon

Photo (p. 29) by Andy Watson, Watson Rodeo Photos,
Inc, Bozeman, Montana.
Photos (p. 31) Umatilla-Morrow ESD staff.

Published by:

Mt. Emily Press
1808 First Street, Suite 3
La Grande, Oregon 97850

Please visit us at www.mtemilypress.com
Activities and school visit information available
at the website.

This book may be ordered from the publisher at
www.mtemilypress.com.

For Rich, Rami & Neil, Garhan & Torri who let me follow my own path, and for Roseletta & Max who inspire me to live in a world rich with laughter and dreams.
—N.G.A.

To my husband Rob and my kids Sarah and James who have not had a home-cooked meal since this project started.
—J.G.M.

Nancy Garhan Attebury

Nancy has penned fifteen educational books for children including *Gloria Steinem: Champion of Women's Rights*, selected for the 2007 Amelia Bloomer List, *Out and About at the United States Mint*, and *Trickster Tales*. Her work has appeared in "Highlights," "Jack and Jill," and "Humpty Dumpty." Exposing children to an appealing regional event is what Nancy hopes to do with *'Twas the Night Before Round-Up*.

Nancy motorcycles and hikes in her spare time. Visit her website at http://attebury.wgeo.org/. Grandpa George Attebury was a Saddle Bronc rider in the 1912 Pendleton Round-Up.

Joan Gilbert Madsen

Joan is a native Oregonian and grew up in La Grande. She attended Eastern Oregon University and received her BFA degree in Art from Oregon State University. Joan currently lives in Enterprise, Oregon with her husband and two kids. She works as a graphic designer/illustrator and can't imagine a more fun career. Joan volunteers bringing art into the local schools and area summer camps.

Joan's relative, Brent Gilbert, was a Bull Rider in the Pendleton Round-Up during the mid-1970s.

We would like to thank Robin, Dawn, Craig, Catherine, Catherine, Jenny and the Enterprise Public Library.

Pendleton Round-Up

A fun-filled event takes place in Pendleton, Oregon every September. It lasts a week and includes a rodeo called the Round-Up. The rodeo began in 1910 and will celebrate its 100th anniversary in 2010. The rodeo is one of the oldest and most important rodeos in the world!

Happy Canyon, a pageant full of Indian tradition, runs each night of the Round-Up. Parades, concerts, dances, barbecues and the Professional Bull Riding Classic are some pre Round-Up festivities held during the week.

To learn more, visit www.pendletonroundup.com. or visit the Hall of Fame Museum in Pendleton, Oregon.

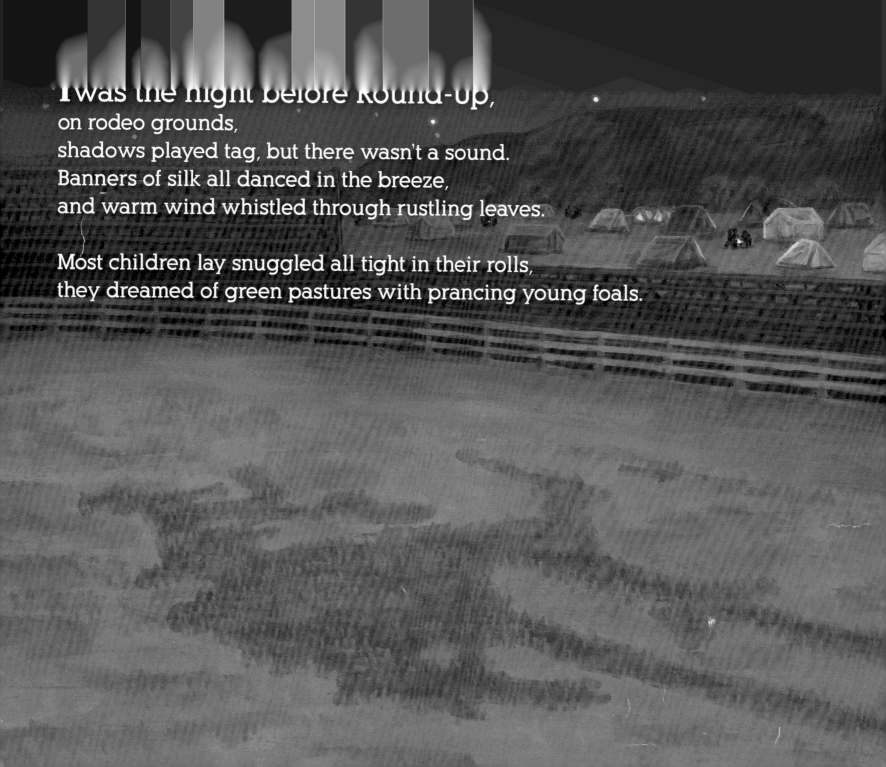

Twas the night before Round-up,
on rodeo grounds,
shadows played tag, but there wasn't a sound.
Banners of silk all danced in the breeze,
and warm wind whistled through rustling leaves.

Most children lay snuggled all tight in their rolls,
they dreamed of green pastures with prancing young foals.

But a tale had been told, it is one we had heard
about horses that sped through the night in a blur.
They lit the show ring with a dazzling sight,
one time a year on pre Round-Up night.

So near the arena,
tucked close to the stands
we cowkids kept pace
with our pre Round-Up plans.

We fluffed up bright 'kerchiefs,
shined boots with a zest,
we tightened our belts
and buttoned our vests.

Then out to the west,
what did we hear,
but thundering hooves
as wild horses drew near.

We climbed up the fence and stared at the sight
as the riderless horses swept in from the night.
They glittered and glistened with silvery tack,
each raced like a jet to one end and back.

Thick dust whirled in circles, we yippee-ki-yayed,
we hooted and yelled for this moon-dust parade.

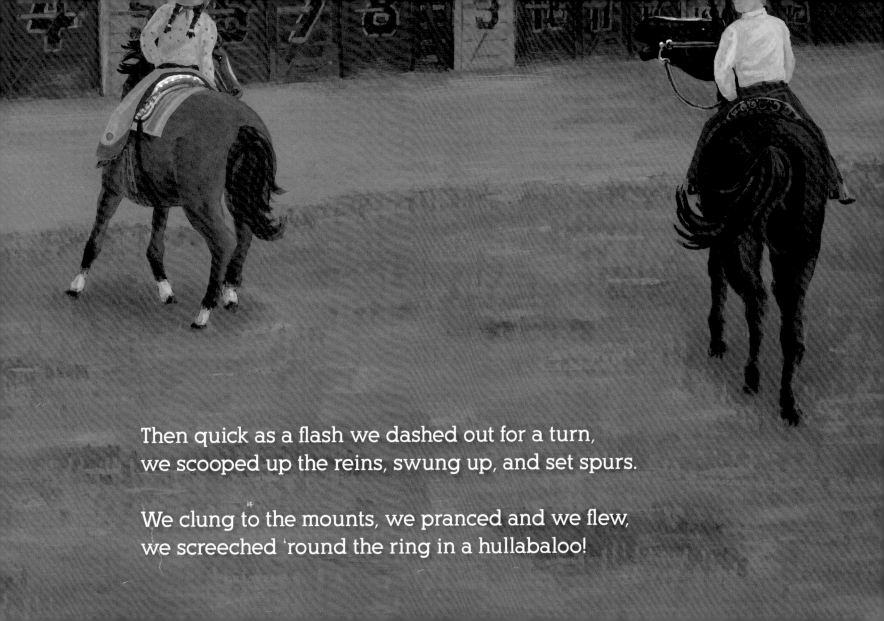

Then quick as a flash we dashed out for a turn,
we scooped up the reins, swung up, and set spurs.

We clung to the mounts, we pranced and we flew,
we screeched 'round the ring in a hullabaloo!

We swept past the barrels,
we skirted the poles,
we showed grace and speed
in our rodeo roles.

The dark sky was bathed
with a soft moonlit glow,
we gripped feisty steeds
in the wildest of shows.

Throughout the arena
we stirred up such clatter
that a throng rushed in
to see what was the matter.
The crowd drew a breath
and held it in tight
when they witnessed the romping
on pre Round-Up night!

We twirled scratchy lassos and tossed them with ease
to snatch bucking doggies (calves, if you please).
We tied spiffy knots, the kind that held firm,
the calves blinked and mooed, they wiggled and squirmed.

The knots held the calves, we hugged them and then,
untied frisky critters who loped back to the pens.

Up next came a race, speed put to the test,
we cowkids choked reins, which horse was the best?
We zipped past the crowd, we rushed and we sped,
we pulled neck and neck, we dashed head to head.
A cyclone sprang up in a spinning brown swirl
when our running raised dust, in a rush and a whirl.

We twirled 'round and 'round, how did we hang on?
By the seat of our pants, we delighted the throng.
In every event we earned perfect scores,
the stands shook and shimmied, the crowd rocked and roared.

We dazzled and charmed, the people were pleased,
now the mounts stamped and pawed, they grew anxious to leave.

But what would we do, should we give up the pace?
Or should we cling tight, and go on with the race?
Well, right then and there we all chose to sit tight,
we bucked and prepared to ride off in the night.

And quick as they came, with a flash and a flurry,
the wild steeds reared up and set off in a hurry.

Run Bullet and Speck, rush Bandit and Flip!
Race Phantom and Blaze, dash Sparky and Zip!
Stir dust by the buckets, and answer the call,
to dash away, fly away, zip away all."

As we charged toward the gate, we waved to the crowd;
we were swift and so brave, we were tough, we were proud.

And our voices rang clear when we rose up in flight,

"Happy Round-Up to all, on this pre Round-Up night!"

Famous Round-Up Animals:

Cataldo was a Paint horse with "medicine hat markings." Cataldo's job was to carry the American flag in opening ceremonies.

Sharkey was a bull that wore a saddle! Riding him was not easy. During one Round-Up he bucked off 36 riders in three days.

War Paint could "Let 'er Buck!" He bucked off 9 out of every 10 riders in the 20 years he worked. He is stuffed and has been in the museum exhibit since 1977. Museum information says War Paint "bucks forever."

Beauregard was a majestic elk. He played a role in the opening scene of Happy Canyon from 1982-2000.

Midnight bucked up a storm in 1969. He could leap 15 feet out of the chute.

"Go Figure"

- If Sharkey bucked off 36 riders in 3 days, how many did he buck off on average in just 1 day?

- Measure 15 feet to see how far Midnight could leap when he left the chute.

- What do you think "medicine hat markings" look like on a horse?

- What name would you give to a horse that bucked fast and high?

- What animal would you pick to be in the Happy Canyon pageant? Why?

- If War Paint bucked off 9 out of every 10 riders, how many did he buck off if 20 riders tried to ride him?

Glossary:

Arena   Place where an event like a rodeo is held

Barrels   Containers set up as turning places for horses

Doggies   Little calves

Foals   Young horses

'Kerchiefs   (Neckerchiefs) Scarves or bandanas for cowboys or cowgirls

Lasso   Rope used to catch horses, calves, or steers

Poles   Sticks used as markers to turn in a pole bending race

Mounts, Steeds   Horses

Reared   Stood up on back legs

Reins   Strips of leather that horse riders grip to control their horses

Spurs   Metal tools strapped to the back of boots used to urge a horse to run faster

Rodeo, Round-Up   Festive contest of horse, steer, bull and calf events

Stands   Place where spectators gather to watch an event

Tack   Saddle, bridle, reins and other gear used to equip a horse

Make It Up:
Use five glossary words from above to make up a story about your day at the Round-Up. Tell where you sat or stood, what you saw, how the contests turned out. Share your story.

Let 'er Buck:
Gather some friends. Make up running and jumping "rodeo events" you can do without horses. Then try them out and have fun!

"The toughest saddle bronc to ride is one that ducks and dives."
—Jake Hayworth, saddle bronc rider

Some Round-Up Contests

Winners win money and may win a silver belt buckle, a fancy horse bit, gold and silver spurs, a trophy, or a saddle!

Saddle Bronc   A saddled horse shoots out of the gate. Its goal is to buck high and dump the rider! A rider aims to stay on eight seconds. The best ride wins.

Bull Riding   A big bull huffs and puffs and bucks and tries to throw off its rider. If it does, the rider scurries to get clear of the mad bull. A rider aims to ride eight seconds. The best ride wins.

Team Roping   Two cowboys, a header and heeler on horses, try to rope a running steer. The header ropes the steer's head or horns. The heeler ropes its heels or back legs. The team that does this fastest wins.

Bareback Riding   Bareback horses wear no saddle. The rider needs to stay on the slick bucking horse for eight seconds and ride well. The best ride wins.

Steer Wrestling   A steer bursts out the gate. A cowboy rides after it. He dives on top of the steer, twists its horns and wrestles it to the ground. The fastest take down wins.

Barrel Racing   Female riders run a pattern around barrels and race back to the starting point. The fastest time wins.

Wild Cow Milking   Contestants catch a wild cow and milk it on the spot.

Calf Roping   A calf breaks from the chute and a cowboy rides after it. The cowboy ropes the calf, jumps off his horse and takes hold of the calf. The cowboy lays the calf on the ground and ties three of its legs together. The cowboy who does this the fastest is the winner.

Steer Roping   This contest is like calf roping but it is done with a steer instead of a calf.

Indian Relay Race   This is a fast-paced race where bareback horses and riders zip around the track. Without coming to a full stop, horses and riders are traded after one time around and keep racing.

Other Events

Happy Canyon This nightly display of Indian pageantry presents a story of how the Pendleton area developed. The flashy show gives the viewpoint of the Indians and the settlers. The show includes people, elk, birds, oxen and horses.

Westward Ho! This rousing parade of covered wagons, carts, buggies, pack trains, ox and mule teams and hundreds of Native Americans in full dress passes through downtown streets.

Children's Day Rodeo Special needs kids compete in this event. They ride a hand-rocked mechanical bull, rope a pretend steer, barrel race on a stick pony, untie a ribbon on a goat, ride a real horse and take a buggy ride. They receive trophies, a neckerchief and a photo with a cowboy or a cowgirl.

"Let 'er Buck! Rope cows... ride horse."
Rian Middleton, Children's Day Rodeo cowkid

Round-Up Time Line

1910	The first Round-Up was held.
1915	The first Happy Canyon show was held.
1924-1925	Wallace Smith drew the "Let 'er Buck" bucking horse.
1929	Bonnie McCarroll was bucked off a bronc and died ten days later. As a result, women contestants were banned for many years.
1940	A fire destroyed the wood grandstands.
1942-1943	The Round-Up was canceled due to WWII.
1957	The Round-Up was televised.
1960	The Dallas Cowboys and L.A. Rams played football on the grass. Rodeo chute #6 was used for the dressing room!
1970s	A movie, "Bull from Sky," was filmed on grounds.
1984	The first Children's Day Rodeo was held.
1990	Women contestants returned to the Round-Up for Barrel Racing.
2000	The Round-Up began raising money for the "Tough Enough to Wear Pink" cancer campaign.
2008	Over $20,000 was raised for the "Tough Enough" campaign.

Melissa McMichael, Children's Rodeo participant, picks up some rope advice.

Color Round-Up

Some cowkid equipment is hiding
in this puzzle. Ask a grown-up
to copy this page for you.
Then color shapes with one dot (.) blue.
Color shapes with 2 dots (. .) red.
Color shapes with 3 dots (. . .) yellow
and see what you discover.

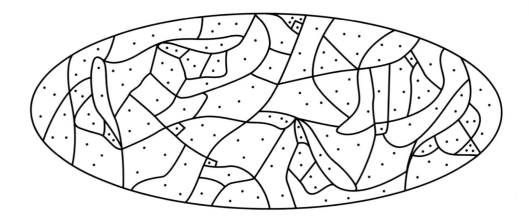

Pole Benders – a super snack for cowkids!

Get ready to race your ponies around the arena and raise a flurry of dust after you fill up on these finger lickers. Making them is easy; eating them is fun, fun, fun!

Use soap and water to wash the dust from your hands before you make this snack.

Materials:
1 table knife	1 cheese cutter	4 wooden skewers broken in half
1 cutting board	1 drinking glass	

Ingredients:
2 sticks of white string cheese	1 small block of yellow cheese
8 black olives	2 strips of red pepper about ½" wide and 2" long

Directions:

1. Use the knife to cut the white string cheese in pieces about ½" long.
2. Cut the yellow cheese in cubes about ½" square.
3. Cut the red pepper strips in pieces about 1" long.
4. Stick 1 piece of white cheese, 1 olive, and 1 yellow cheese cube on a skewer.
5. Repeat the pattern on the same skewer and add a strip of pepper at the top for a flag.
6. Stand each snack in the drinking glass until you have 8 Pole Bender snacks.
7. Then enjoy your treats!

For more activities and information about school visits go to www.mtemilypress.com